More Stories Huey Tells

More Stories Huey Tells

ANN CAMERON

Pictures by **LIS TOFT**

Frances Foster Books

Farrar, Straus and Giroux • New York

Library of Congress Cataloging-in-Publication Data
Cameron, Ann, date.
More stories Huey tells / Ann Cameron ; pictures by Lis Toft. —
1st ed.
    p.   cm.
"Frances Foster books."
Summary: Huey, his older brother Julian, and their family and
friends plant a garden, play basketball, try to get Huey's father to
stop smoking, learn about the universe, and more.
ISBN 0-374-35065-5
[1. Brothers—Fiction.   2. Family life—Fiction.   3. Afro-
Americans—Fiction.]   I. Toft, Lis, ill.   II. Title.
PZ7.C1427Mn   1997
[Fic]—dc20   96-18420

To Gwen Boozé with love

I thank Eric Chipman,
the astronomer who led the team for scheduling the
first year of observations by the Hubble Space Telescope,
for seeing that the astronomical information in
"The Night I Turned Fifteen Billion" reflects
current observations and theories.

Contents

More Stories Huey Tells

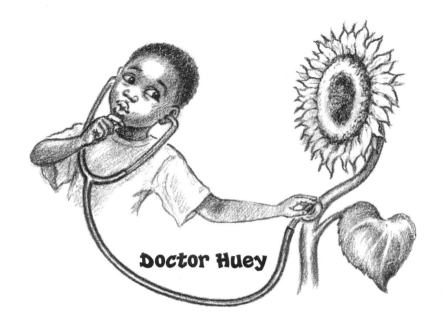

Doctor Huey

I made a special place in our yard. It was a sunflower forest. I grew it.

In the rest of the garden there were other things. My brother, Julian, planted a rose-bush. Our friend Gloria planted some tomato plants—some for us, and some for her because she doesn't have space for a garden at home. We had corn and beans and cucumbers and melons, too. My sunflowers were at the back of the garden, where they wouldn't shade the other plants. Of everything in the garden, they were best of all.

I planted tiny black-and-white-striped seeds—twelve of them in two rows, the way my dad told me. I put white plastic markers in the ground by each seed, so I wouldn't forget where they were. And then I watered around the markers every day.

In a week, two tiny green leaves had sprouted by each marker. They looked like green tongues licking at the light. They grew fast and got strong.

When we planted the garden, we'd started tying my dog, Spunky, on a rope so he wouldn't get into it and step on the plants. When my sunflowers got four leaves, I untied him and took him on his leash to show him my sunflower plants. He just sniffed them and didn't hurt them, so my dad said

Spunky didn't have to be tied up anymore, and he could be in the garden with us.

Everything in the garden was changing, but my plants were changing most of all. They were changing into giants.

In a month, they were taller than me. In another week, they were taller than my brother, Julian, and my friend Gloria, and much taller than Julian's rosebush.

One day, when I took Spunky to the sunflowers, he got between the rows and sat down. So I did, too. It was wonderful sitting among the sunflowers. They had big, rough green leaves shaped like hearts. They looked like they rained valentines. And they had big stalks, almost as big as tree trunks.

"It's nice here! It's like being in a rain forest!" I shouted to Gloria and Julian. They came over and sat down with Spunky and me. They thought it was like a rain forest, too. After that, the three of us started to play there, and we played there almost all summer long.

We made roads under the sunflowers and raced cars. We played marbles under them. In another month, my sunflowers had enormous yellow flowers with dark centers. By then Julian was bringing Mom roses from his rosebush to put in a vase, but I couldn't do that with my sunflowers. The smallest ones were bigger than dinner plates. The biggest ones were giants, like big truck hubcaps. And they moved! Not too much, but a little bit every day, following the sun.

By August, the sunflower plants were taller than my dad. Julian, Gloria, and I tied strings between the stalks and hung some old sheets on them to make walls in the rain for-

est. The light looked green in our rain forest room.

I was proud.

Then one morning, Gloria came over. Julian and Spunky and I were in the rain forest, but Gloria said she didn't want to stay.

"Why not?" I said.

"It's not nice anymore," she said.

"What do you mean?" I said.

"It's not pretty," Gloria said.

Julian looked up. "Gloria's right," he said. "It's not nice anymore."

"I think it's nice!" I said.

"All the leaves are droopy," Gloria said.

"The flower petals are half off, Huey," Julian said. "Anyone can see that!"

I looked up through the sunflower branches. Anybody *could* see it. The heart-shaped leaves that used to stand up like umbrellas were flopped down like old rags. The flower petals were stained-looking and all messed up.

"It's still the best place," I said.

"It *was*," Julian said. "It was a real nice place."

"I'd rather play at my house," Gloria said.

"Me too," Julian said.

"Don't you want to stay and fix it up? Don't you want to make it better?"

"No," Julian said.

"Do you want to go with us?" Gloria asked.

"No," I said.

"Well, I hope you can fix it," Gloria said.

She and Julian left.

"Stay!" I said to Spunky. He stayed. "You still like it here, don't you?" I said. He thumped his tail on the bare ground, and I patted him.

I studied the sunflower rain forest. I didn't like what I saw. The big sunflower stalks were turning brown. When I stood up and looked at the centers of the flowers, I could see they weren't the same brown they used to be. They used to be a velvety brown, and now they were dead-looking.

"Spunky, they're sick!" I said. "What do they need?"

He didn't answer. I guessed he didn't know much about plants. Probably he never had a garden before.

"I planted them. I watered them. I made them grow. I can make them well!" I told Spunky.

I looked at the sunflowers. "Don't worry," I said. "I'll save you!"

If my mom and dad had been home, I would have asked them how to do it. But

they weren't. I tried to remember everything I knew about plants. The words "plant food" came into my mind. But I wasn't sure what plant food was.

Plants' leaves make sugar, my dad had told me. But I could see the sunflowers' leaves probably weren't making sugar anymore. The whole plant probably needed sugar.

"Come, Spunky!" I said.

We ran into the house. In the kitchen cupboard there was a five-pound bag of sugar. It was practically full. I took it out to the garden. I spread the whole bag around the roots of my twelve sunflower plants.

"What do you think, Spunky?" I said. "That's a lot better, isn't it?"

Spunky wagged his tail.

But when I looked at the mangled-up sunflower blossoms, I thought maybe sugar wasn't enough.

In the morning when my dad gets up, he always has to have coffee. He says it's a waker-upper, and he can't wake up without it. He says once he drinks it, he can do all the things he needs to do—count all his bones and make sure none are missing, open his eyes a little bit at a time, and start breathing.

It looked like the sunflowers needed to start breathing.

"Come, Spunky!" I said. We ran back to the house.

There was an almost full two-pound can of coffee in the kitchen cupboard. I took it all and spread it around my sunflowers. They looked a little better, I thought.

Plants needed minerals. That's something my dad had said.

I didn't know where to get any. But then I remembered.

"Come, Spunky!" I said.

We ran back to the house. In the kitchen cupboard right next to the sink there was a bottle labeled VITAMIN-MINERAL SUPPLEMENT. Dad never said plants needed vitamins. He only mentioned minerals. But I figured vitamins couldn't hurt. I gave each plant five vitamin-mineral pills. I used the garden trowel and buried the tablets next to the stalks. The twelfth sunflower only got three pills, though, because there weren't any more.

"How are you doing?" I said to the sunflowers.

They looked at me like hospital patients in old green gowns, and their big battered heads all nodded.

"There's hope!" I said.

I thought about plants some more.

In school, I'd found out that when Native Americans planted corn, they used to put chopped-up pieces of fish in the mounds where they planted it, to help it grow.

"Come, Spunky!" I said.

We ran back into the house. I didn't have time to catch fish to feed my sunflowers. It could take years for me to catch enough.

But in the kitchen cupboard there were three cans of tuna fish. I opened them with

the can opener and took them all outside. With the hoe, I dug down a little under the sugar and the coffee and made kind of a well. I put tuna fish in each well and covered it up. There wasn't very much tuna fish for each hole. But it was all I had.

I tried to think of something else to give my rain forest, but I couldn't. It was hard to think because my hands smelled so much of tuna fish. I let Spunky lick them off.

My mom says you shouldn't take medicine unless you really need it, and then you shouldn't take too much. Too many medicines might get the sunflowers confused. Probably I had done enough.

I went to the faucet and washed my hands, and washed up all the empty bottles and cans and put them in the recycling box on the porch. Then I pulled the garden hose over to the sunflowers and watered them till they were really flooded. The coffee got sopping wet, and the sugar dissolved completely.

"Come, Spunky!" I said. We went back to the faucet and turned the water off. Then we sat down a little way from the sunflowers, on the grass, where it wasn't wet.

I thought the sunflowers were getting better. Some of the leaves didn't look so droopy. But I couldn't remember if they were the same leaves that didn't look droopy before the medicine.

I remembered one more thing I'd heard. Plants like music. If you play music for them, they grow better. It's a scientific fact. That's what somebody said, I don't know who.

I don't have a radio, but Julian does. And it runs on batteries.

"Come, Spunky!" I said.

We ran into the house and up to Julian's and my room. I found Julian's yellow radio and brought it outside. I figured the best music to play would be peaceful music. I pointed the speakers at the sunflowers and turned on peaceful music loud for them. Spunky and I sat down and watched them. After a while Spunky yawned, and I got very sleepy myself . . .

"HUUU-EYY! HUUU-EYY!" It was my mom's voice. The music wasn't playing any-more. No sound was coming from Julian's yellow radio. I guessed I'd been asleep. I didn't want to leave my sunflowers, but I fig-ured I'd better.

"Come, Spunky!" I said, and we walked slowly to the house.

My mom and dad and Julian were in the

kitchen, and lunch was on the table. It was egg salad for sandwiches. It looked kind of watery.

We all sat down. Spunky lay down under the table.

"Sorry I didn't have enough eggs for a really good egg salad," my mom apologized. "I was going to make tuna salad. I thought I had three cans—but there wasn't even one!"

"That's strange," my dad said. "I was going to make myself iced coffee, but the coffee was gone. And the sugar was missing, too."

"I went to take my vitamin," Mom said, "but the bottle is gone."

"I was going to play my radio," Julian said, "but it's not in my room."

"Have you noticed anything missing, Huey?" my mom asked.

"No," I said.

Everybody looked at me.

"Those things aren't really missing. I just— used them."

Everybody yelled. "You *whaaat*?"

"Used things. For medicine for the sunflowers," I explained. "They're sick. I'll show you."

Mom, Dad, and Julian followed me out to the garden. There was still a little lake of muddy water around the sunflowers. I picked up Julian's radio off the grass and gave it to him.

He tried to turn it on, and found out it was already on. He looked angry.

"It's perfect," I told him. "I didn't do anything to it! It's just like new. Only it doesn't make any sound anymore. That's all."

My dad took the radio. He held it to his ear

and shook it. It still didn't make any sound.

"I think it's okay," my dad said. "I think it's just that the batteries are dead."

"I was playing music for the sunflowers. It played for a long time," I explained. "Sorry."

"And the other medicines?" my dad said. "Where are they?"

"Buried," I said, "or dissolved. I ran a lot of water."

"I can see that," my dad said.

"Please," I said, "can you tell me what's the matter with my sunflowers? Why are they sick?"

My mom and dad looked at them across the muddy water lake.

"Huey," my mom said, "these plants aren't sick—they're dying."

"Dying!" I said. "Why? I took care of them. I did my best."

"They're dying because it's time, Huey," my mother said. "They're annual plants: they live just one season, and then they die."

"Nobody told me they were going to die!" I said.

"I thought you knew," my dad said.

I rubbed my eyes. I almost cried.

"Look, Huey," my mom said. "See the inside of the flowers: all that brown stuff is the seeds they've made: their babies, the flowers for next year."

My dad reached out across the wet ground and pulled a flower down to me.

"Look up close," he said.

I did. All the centers of the flowers were tight with seeds. There were hundreds of them in just one flower—packed tighter and neater than anyone ever packed things in a store.

"They really know how to make seeds," I said. Somehow that made me feel a little better.

We went back in the house. I got a lecture about: Ask before you take things. Also about: Ask before you take Julian's things. Dad found some new batteries for Julian's radio, but he said I had to pay out of my allowance for the new set.

I did all the dishes by myself. Julian didn't have to help. My mom said so.

She came back in the kitchen when I was done.

"I'm sorry I wasted stuff," I said. "I wanted to save the sunflowers. But it didn't work."

"Huey," my mom said, "you can still save them."

"I can?" I felt like a doctor again.

"Get the ladder," she said, "and set it up so you can pull some seeds out of each flower head. Then set the seeds on a plate on the porch so they will dry. Next year, you can plant them."

"Come, Spunky!" I said.

We went outside. I got the ladder and took it over to the sunflowers. It kind of sunk in where the big puddle-lake was, but it stayed steady when I climbed it.

I took lots of seeds from every plant and put them in a bag. That still left lots in the flowers for the birds to eat.

I held the last bunch I collected out to the big messed-up heads of all the flowers.

"See?" I said. "I told you I was going to save you, and I have."

Julian on His Birthday

"Happy birthday, ha-ap-py birthday to me-e-e! HAP-PY-Y-Y!" My brother was conducting the song with his fork. Birthday cake crumbs were dropping off it. A big gob of frosting was ready to fall.

"Julian!" my dad said.

Julian stopped swinging his fork. The frosting gob fell.

My dog, Spunky, was right on the job. He caught the frosting gob and swallowed it.

Then he sat back down between us. That's the way Spunky is. Always helping.

Julian didn't even notice.

"Julian," my dad said, "we already sang you 'Happy Birthday.' Wasn't that enough?"

Julian stopped singing. "Almost," he said. He had a goofy smile on his face.

I knew why. On his birthday, eating birthday cake makes Julian crazy. It blinds his eyes. It swells up his head.

It happens every year. After the first bite of birthday cake, he gets a silly grin. After the second bite, he acts like somebody on TV. After the third bite, he thinks he's better than everybody. Especially me.

"Julian, it's time for your presents," my mom said. "Huey, would you bring them out?"

Spunky went with me. We got the presents out of the living room closet. There were two packages, a big one from Mom and Dad and a small one from me.

I knew what they were. The small one from me, socks. The big one from Mom and Dad, sports shoes. Julian could have had a birthday party with fifteen kids, but he chose expensive shoes instead.

I set the packages on the table. Julian opened the big one first and pulled his shoes out of the box—silver and black, with red

lightning stripes and red heel reflectors.

"Superb Athlete Airstream Energy-Cushioned Molecular-Powered Hi-Action Shoes!" he said. "Madness!"

"Madness" is what the kids in his grade say when they think something is cool.

"Open the other one!" I said.

Julian opened the next package—my present, white socks with red, blue, and yellow stripes.

"Nice!" Julian said.

He took off his old socks and shoes. He put on his new ones. He stood up and jumped high.

"Superb Athlete shoes *are* energy-cushioned," he said. "They really, really are!"

"There's one more present," my mom said. She went to get it from wherever she'd had it hidden, came back, and held it out to Julian.

"A basketball!" Julian said.

"This present isn't all yours, though," my mom warned. "It's to share with Huey. You'll remember that, won't you?"

"Da-da-da-*da*!" Julian said. "Happy birthday to me!" He bounced the ball once on the kitchen floor.

"Julian!" my mom said. "You remember no playing ball in the house! You remember about sharing!"

"Yes, Mom," he said.

"Come on outside, boys," my dad said. "I want to show you something."

We all went outside. Spunky lay down on the grass. The rest of us looked where Dad was pointing.

On the garage wall there was a brand-new orange basketball hoop with a net.

"That's for both you boys," my dad said.

"Madness!" Julian said. He made a high toss with our new basketball. It missed the hoop.

Julian ran and got the ball. He looked angry. He retied his new shoes and stubbed the toes at the ground.

I was standing where he could throw it to me, but he didn't even look my way.

"Julian, I want a turn!" I said.

"A basket for me first," Julian said. "Then it will be your turn."

"It should be my turn *now*," I said.

"It's *my* birthday!" Julian said.

I looked at my mom and dad.

"Julian," my dad said, "it's your birthday, but give Huey a chance, too. That basketball hoop is half yours and half Huey's—got that?"

"Yes, sir," Julian said—but he didn't pass the ball to me.

"Your mom and I have a meeting," my dad said. "We'll be back in an hour. Get in some practice while we're gone. And I mean Huey, too."

My dad started for the truck. Then he turned back.

"Lend me that basketball?" he asked.

It was a miracle—Julian heard him and tossed him the ball.

My dad threw high, from a long way off.

The ball soared up and floated. It dropped clean, right through the hoop, just swishing the net.

"Wow!" said Julian. "Madness!"

"Luck," said my dad. "And practice. I'll play some with you boys when we get back."

My mom and dad drove away. Julian took the ball and dribbled it down the driveway. He threw from really close. The ball almost

went in. He threw another one. It wound around the hoop, wobbled, and went in.

But not like the basket Dad made. When Dad threw the ball, it looked like it just had to do whatever he wanted. It flew like a bird. When Julian threw the ball, it looked like it was undecided till the last second.

"A basket!" Julian said. "Madness!"

"Let me try! I can do it!" I said.

"It's not that easy, Huey. It takes lots of practice. Wait awhile."

Julian backed down the driveway, hugging the ball to his body. "I'm going to come in for another basket," he shouted. "Try and stop me! Block me! Try to get the ball away!"

I jumped in front of him and reached for the ball.

He held it high.

"Jump!" he said.

I did, but I couldn't reach it.

Julian tried for another basket and missed. He kicked at the ground with his new shoes. If he kept doing that, he was really going to mess them up.

"When is it my turn?" I asked. "I want a turn to make baskets, too." But Julian was running; he wasn't listening to me.

"Block me again, Huey," he said. "Jump high! Raise your arms more! Can't you jump any higher than that?"

I jumped high, and Julian knocked me over. Spunky growled. I got up.

"Julian! I jumped as high as I can jump, and I'm done jumping when you say jump!"

Julian bounced the ball down the driveway toward the street again.

"Julian, the basketball's not just for you!" I shouted. "Mom said so. The hoop's not just for you either. Dad said so."

"Right now it's still my turn."

I figured I could make a basket. But I wasn't going to get a chance.

I was disgusted. I gave up looking at Julian. I started looking at the basketball hoop. I noticed how it was made. Two metal supports came out from the rim and attached to the wall of the garage.

If a person could throw a string over the hoop next to a support, maybe the support would hold the string in place. A person would have to have a weight on the end of the string to throw it right. A heavy bolt could be a good weight.

I went in the house and downstairs to Dad's workshop. On his workbench, I found a heavy bolt and a roll of thick string. I tied the loose end of the string to the bolt. I took it outside. In back of the house, I let out a bunch of string and practiced throwing the bolt high. I got good at it.

I went to the garage. Julian was almost out in the street, bouncing the basketball under his leg. I didn't go near him. I stood at the side of the basketball hoop. I let out a lot of string and threw the bolt high. I was lucky. The bolt sailed up over the basket the first time, and the string fell over the rim. I ran forward under the basket and picked up the bolt.

I had the string by both ends. I walked backward, and it caught against the support and pulled tight. The top crossed the middle of the hoop straight as a ruler.

I kept letting out string and walking backward, till I was off the driveway and in the yard.

Julian was a long way back. He was

crouching and zigzagging and whirling, dribbling tight like five guys were on him, trying to take the ball away. Then he started coming up the driveway fast. He got near the basket and leaped high. "Madness!" he shouted. "—What is that?"

"String," I said.

"Take it off! I can't shoot a basket with that string over the hoop."

"Why not?" I asked.

"Don't you know *anything*?" Julian asked. "The ball can't go in!"

"It's my basketball hoop, too," I said. "It's half mine. And I'm using my half for string."

Julian walked up on the grass. He looked like he wanted to shove me. I braced my legs and protected my string with my arms. Spunky walked over and growled.

"Remember what Mom said. Remember what Dad said," I told him.

Julian didn't shove me. He shrugged.

"You are so ignorant!" he said.

He dropped the new basketball, and it rolled onto the grass. He went into the garage and came out with our old scuffed softball.

I stayed where I was and held my strings tight. It was like holding the reins on an iron horse. Julian threw the softball through his half of the basketball hoop. It got through the net and dropped out. Julian picked it up. He made another basket from close up. He was good at it. The only trouble was, the softball wouldn't bounce for him.

I got tired of holding the string, but I kept on.

A boy came down the sidewalk. I didn't know him. He stood out at the end of the driveway, watching us.

After a while Julian noticed him.

The boy shouted, "Is that a new game?"

"Right!" I shouted.

"I just moved here," the boy said. "Can I watch?"

"Guess so," Julian said.

The boy came up to us. He looked to be Julian's age, but he was taller than Julian.

"My name's Shavaun. I'd like to try that

game. Nobody played that where I come from."

"My name's Julian," Julian said, "and that's my brother, Huey."

He handed Shavaun the softball. Shavaun threw it, and it dropped through my half of the basket and rolled out of the net. Julian picked up the ball.

"Pretty cool," Shavaun said.

"Madness," Julian said.

Shavaun pointed a thumb at me.

"Your brother's nice to hold the string like that for you."

Julian made a strange face. "He's doing it specially—because it's my birthday."

"Happy birthday!" Shavaun said to Julian. He looked at Julian's feet. "Hey, you got Superb Athlete shoes!" he said.

Julian handed Shavaun the softball and sat

down on the grass. He bent back the tongue of one of his Superb Athlete shoes. There was tiny writing on the inside in fine red silk threads.

" 'Superb Athlete shoes guarantee superior performance of any sport,' " Julian read. "But they don't. I got 'em for my birthday, but I wish I'd had a big party instead."

"They're cool, though," Shavaun said. "If I could choose, I'd rather have Superb Athlete shoes than any party."

Shavaun looked at the basketball hoop and then at me. "Hey," he said, "do you guys think it would be fun to just play regular basketball for a while?"

"Okay with me," Julian said.

"Okay," I said. "Even turns. My turn first."

Julian lent me his knife. I cut the string and pulled it off the basketball hoop. I put the cut

string and the bolt and the roll of string in my pocket—just in case I needed it another time.

Shavaun tossed me the basketball.

"Five tries each," I said.

"Okay," Julian said.

"Okay," Shavaun said.

For a minute, I set the ball on the ground between my feet. I swung my arms and opened and closed my hands to relax them. It had been hard work holding the string tight.

I picked up the new ball and bounced it. The ball felt good and springy. I jogged up to where the free-throw line would be, if there were one. I looked at Spunky. He was watching. I felt steady and more than ready. Slowly, very carefully, I aimed the ball and threw.

It curved up like a rainbow. It dropped like it was looking for a pot of gold.

"Yipes!" Julian said. "A basket!"

"Huey, you've got talent," Shavaun said.

"I knew I could do it," I said. "All I ever needed was a chance."

The False Friend

In a school assembly, I saw a movie about smoke—smoke from factories, smoke from cars, smoke from cigarettes.

Part of the movie was a cartoon. It showed little oxygen-molecule guys. They were the good guys, and they had tickets for a ski lift. They got in the ski lift chairs and went around and around—the way they do in your blood, the movie said.

But then some bad guys came—a gang of

carbon monoxide molecules. They didn't have any tickets. They just muscled up and pushed the oxygen molecules out of the ski lift chairs and sat in their places.

Then at the top of the mountain you could see these other guys, little bubble-snowflake guys that were like human body cells. They were swaying and shriveling up and pounding their sides with their hands and shouting, "Help us! Help us! Oxygen! We need oxygen!"

A whole new bunch of oxygen good guys heard. They ran up and tried to stop the ski lift and push the carbon monoxide gang out of their chairs. But the carbon monoxide bad guys just kicked them and kept on riding. At the top of the hill, the bubble-snowflake body-cell guys started falling over dead.

The good guys lost. It was horrible.

After the movie, I walked home from school with Julian.

"Julian, is it true those carbon monoxide things are in cigarettes and can go into your blood?"

"For sure," Julian said.

"It's true they can keep you from getting oxygen?"

"Yup," Julian said.

"Is it true a person's heart can break down if it doesn't get oxygen?"

"Right," Julian said.

"Then why does Dad smoke?" I asked.

"I don't know," Julian said.

"We should make him quit! We should *kill* those cigarettes!" I said.

"Right!" Julian said.

So we planned a way to do it.

·   ·   ·

My dad was taking a catnap in his chair when we found the cigarettes in his pocket.

We didn't put the whole pack down the toilet at once. That could have stopped it up. We broke the cigarettes in pieces and flushed them down two at a time. After that, we tore up the cardboard pack and threw it in the wastebasket. Then we went out to play.

When we came inside, my dad was awake. He was prowling around the living room like a panther, lifting up newspapers, looking behind plants, pulling back the curtains, and sticking his hand deep down behind the cushions in the couch. My mom was watching him.

We watched him, too. We didn't ask what he was doing. We knew.

"I brought a whole new pack home with me, I'm sure I did. Darned if I know where they went."

He saw us. "If you boys wanted to be helpful," he said, "you'd look for my cigarettes."

We didn't say anything. We didn't move.

My dad looked bothered. He stared at us. He got down on his knees and looked under the couch.

"You aren't going to find them," Julian said.

My dad jumped up and glowered at us. "Why not?" he said.

"We took them," I said.

"You *what*!" my dad said. "You *took* my cigarettes! Give them back right now!"

Julian looked nervous. "We can't," he said.

"Where *are* they?" my dad demanded.

"On the way to the sewer," Julian said.

"They went down the toilet," I said.

My dad stormed over to us.

"They didn't *go* down the toilet!" my dad said. "Cigarettes don't just walk off and jump into the toilet and drown. You *put them* there. And that is *stealing*!"

"They're bad for you!" I said.

"We're glad we did it," Julian said.

"You *stole* from your own father!" my dad said. He was boiling mad.

"Ralph, don't be so harsh," my mom said.

"We didn't take them to steal. We did it to help you," Julian said.

"We want you to quit smoking," I said.

"*My* smoking is *my* business!" my dad said. "And if you *ever* take my cigarettes again, I promise you, you boys won't like what I will do."

We didn't say anything. We just walked away.

At night, when we were supposed to be in bed, we listened on the stairway to my dad talking to my mom.

"Taking my cigarettes—that wasn't right!" my dad was saying. "Taking things is not the way to fix a problem. The boys had better not do it again."

My mom said, "I'm pretty sure they won't do it again."

"Good!" my dad said.

"They won't do it again because you are older and bigger and stronger than they are, and you threatened them. Threatening people is not a good way to solve problems either.

"And about your smoking, Ralph—you know they're right."

·   ·   ·

We were in the living room. We were going to have a family talk about smoking.

"I know you're scared about it," my dad said.

"We're afraid you're going to die from it," I said. "We want you to stop."

"You're asking something very hard," my dad said. "I'm not sure I *can* stop."

"You can't stop?" Julian said. He sounded horrified.

"Julian! Don't sound like that! Huey! Don't look so scared!"

"We're scared you're going to die," I said.

"People *do* die from smoking," my dad admitted. "But mostly when they're old. I'm still young. Besides, I don't smoke *very* much. I don't smoke at night when I'm sleeping, or when I'm shaving, or at meals. Mostly I just smoke at work.

"A lot of people smoke like furnaces till they're ninety or a hundred years old. And then they die from something else, like slipping in the bathtub."

My mom rolled her eyes. "If as many died from slipping in the bathtub as die from cigarettes, nobody would ever take a bath," she said.

"Ralph, I know you're right about still being young. You aren't going to die tomorrow from cigarettes. But the boys are right, too. Smoking is dangerous."

My dad sighed. "I've been doing it a long time," he said.

"How long?" Julian demanded.

"I started when I was fifteen."

"Why did you do it?" I asked.

"It made me feel grownup," Dad said. "Sometimes I went to parties. I felt alone.

When I smoked, I felt like I had a friend in my hand."

Julian and I looked at each other. We didn't know what to say.

"Now I don't feel lonesome, and I am grownup. But I still can't give up my friend."

"A lousy, terrible, awful friend!" Julian said.

"Well, sometimes a person gets a false friend," Dad said. "A friend you want to be with even if he leads you wrong. Cigarettes are my false friend."

Dad touched the big ashtray he used. "For you all," he said, "I'll get rid of this. When I smoke at home, I can go outside to do it. That way you all won't have to breathe the bad air, too—but that doesn't mean I'm stopping!"

"Could you cut down?" my mom asked.

My dad thought a long time. "Perhaps," he said. "Probably."

"Maybe it would help you," my mom said, "if you counted how many cigarettes each day and told the boys. Then the boys could mark it on a calendar so you could have a record of how many you smoke."

"They don't need to do that," Dad said.

Mom smiled. "Maybe it will help them," she said, "even if it doesn't help you."

My dad made a face. "If you want to do it, boys, it's all right with me."

That night, before we went to bed, Dad smoked his last cigarette for the day and told us the count—forty-two. We drew forty-two skulls and taped them on the kitchen calendar for that day.

"Skulls!" my dad said. "I thought you were just going to write down the number. Drawing skulls is completely unnecessary. I don't want to look at that!"

Julian thought about it. "From now on," he said, "we'll only draw a skull if you smoke more than the day before. If you smoke less, we'll draw a happy face."

"All right," Dad said.

Every night, Dad smoked outside. He kept an old tin can right outside the kitchen door to put his cigarette butts in.

He wouldn't let us go out with him when he went out to smoke, but my dog, Spunky, went out with him. Spunky looked worried when Dad got up to go outside, as if he knew something was wrong. And every time Dad went out to smoke, I felt sad. I wondered if he felt alone, the way he had when he was a teenager. I wondered if he felt grownup.

Each night before we went to bed, Dad smoked his last cigarette for the day. Then he told us the total, and we wrote it on the kitchen calendar. When the total went down from the day before, we drew a happy face by the number. When it went up, we drew a skull.

The count never went back up to forty-two. The second day it was thirty-nine.

"I'm working to make it go down," Dad told us. "I just get real edgy when I don't smoke. I feel like I *have* to do it."

Two months went by. My mom packed up

carrots for Dad to take to work so he could eat them instead of smoking. She told him she used to smoke. To quit, she yelled at cigarettes and told them she hated them. But Dad said that wouldn't work for him.

He didn't yell at cigarettes, but he sure yelled at us a lot—sometimes for almost nothing. Once, after he did it, I told my

mom, "Dad was nicer when he smoked more!"

"Don't say that!" she told me. "Dad's body is addicted to cigarettes. It keeps telling him to smoke, and he has to say no to it, all day long. It's hard. It makes him cranky. Please, Huey, don't get cross when he gets cross. Try to show him you love him."

The number of cigarettes Dad smoked each day got all the way down to ten. And then it just stayed at ten—every day the same. And it seemed like Dad never even looked at our calendar anymore.

One night, we decided to mark a skull by the ten.

"Probably Dad won't even notice," Julian said.

But he was wrong. Dad saw it the minute we put it there.

"How come there's a skull by the ten?" he complained. He said it as if we were teachers who weren't being fair.

"Ten is too many," Julian said.

"We want you to quit smoking," I said.

"Quitting is too much!" He paused. "The truth is," he said softly, "I still love my false friend."

We felt terrible. We didn't even want to look at him.

"Julian and Huey," my dad said, "don't be like that! Come in the living room. Sit down with me."

So we did.

"Listen," my dad said. "This tobacco fight isn't happening to you. You think it is—but it isn't. You'll never understand it unless you have to go through it—and I hope you never do."

Julian and I looked at each other. "We think we do understand," Julian said.

"Maybe you do understand, then! Maybe you understand and I don't!" My dad sounded angry, but then he spoke softer.

"Sometimes I feel strange. I feel there's something more I have to learn—something I have to learn so I can change the way I think."

"Like what?" I asked.

"I don't know." My dad spread his hands as if something invisible was falling from them and he was staring at it as it hit the rug.

He looked at us. "There's something you boys need to learn, too, and it's very important. Sometimes in life, people are going to fail you. They don't want to, they don't mean to, but they will. Even people you love. But if someone fails you, don't you ever get mixed up and think because he failed, *you've* failed."

He looked embarrassed. "I mean—me. I'm talking about me. You've been trying to help me, and you've helped. Don't blame *yourselves* for what I can't do. I'm not perfect, and I never will be. But I love you."

He wrapped his arms around us and hugged us, and we hugged him back.

When we went up to bed, I asked Julian, "Do you think we should stop marking the calendar?"

"No," Julian said. "Not yet."

And we agreed. As long as we could maybe help our dad, we'd never give up.

The Night I Turned Fifteen Billion

Dad was wearing the party hat we'd fixed for him. It was made out of white paper with lots of glitter glued on it. We had drawn two big A's on it with a blue marker, and all around them we'd painted gold stars and yellow comets and lots of colored spirals that my mom said were the shapes of some galaxies the stars are in.

We—my family, plus my dog, Spunky, and our friends Gloria, Shavaun, and Shavaun's brother, Tyrone—were having a party for Dad in our yard. He had just got an A in his first college course—an astronomy class. He took the class to learn about the universe. Besides, he told us, every minute he'd think about astronomy would be one less minute trying not to think about smoking cigarettes.

Astronomy is the study of the stars. That's why we put stars and comets and galaxies on Dad's hat. We were having the party at twilight, so later we could sit on the blankets we had spread out in the yard and watch the stars come out.

First we played a game we made up called meteor tag. If the person who was It tagged us before we got to the blankets, we were "out"—vaporized by the earth's atmosphere. If we got back to the blankets, we were meteors landed on Earth. When Dad was It, he

chased us all over the yard, and we dived into the blankets just like meteors landing. If he hadn't slowed down to hold on to his party hat, and if Spunky hadn't run in front of him, he would have vaporized us every time.

After a while we got tired, and hungry, too. Then Gloria and Julian and I went into the kitchen for the star-shaped cookies and the special punch we'd made. "Milky Way Galactic Punch" is what we called it. We made it out of milk, because of the name of the galaxy Earth is in—the Milky Way. Julian put lots of shredded coconut in it to be star dust and comets and meteors. I put in lots of ice to be empty space, and butterscotch chips to be the stars.

I carried the biggest glass of all to my dad and explained what all the stuff in it was supposed to be. He swallowed some. "Very good!" he said. "Very chewy—but very galactic."

We all got in a circle around Dad, and Julian gave a toast in his honor. "To Dad, a student of the universe!" he said. We clinked glasses.

"Thank you," Dad said. "I wasn't sure I could learn so much stuff—but I did it!" He lifted his special hat and bowed.

Above us, the sky was getting dark. I saw one star, and then I saw more and more—just like they were showing up for the party. The sky got velvety black. We lay on our backs on the blankets and used Gloria's binoculars to look at the stars.

"There are hundreds!" Shavaun said.

"Maybe more!" Gloria said.

I looked. "There are *lots*," I said.

I tried to show the stars to Spunky through

the binoculars. Maybe he needed special dog binoculars, because he kept trying to look down at the grass.

"There are billions more stars than we can see," Dad said. "My professor said there are a thousand billion, just in our galaxy."

Shavaun shaded his eyes with his hands and stared upward. "How does he know?" he asked. "Seems like it could take a person's whole life to count to a thousand billion. No time out for lunch or holidays, no movies, no baseball games. Nothing. And then, suppose you got to be seven hundred years old, and you'd counted to five hundred billion, and your brother or somebody interrupted you and you had to start counting over? Even if you'd been friends 695 years, you'd want to break his head!"

"No astronomer's counted the stars one by one," Dad explained. "No human being could do it. What astronomers have done is count the stars in one little part of a galaxy. Then they estimate how much bigger a galaxy is than the little part where they counted, and how many galaxies there are, and how big the universe is. Then they do some multiplying. That's how they number the stars. They can't do it exactly. They just make their best guess."

We were silent, just flattening ourselves to the grass and looking up and up and up.

"Way, way up there somewhere there might be people," Gloria said.

"My professor said there are a billion trillion planets," Dad said. "Out of so many, some must be like Earth . . ."

"Way far from here," my mom said quietly, "right this minute, some creatures kind of like us are probably out in their yard having a party, looking across the universe and wondering if we exist."

"Why can't we see them? Why can't they see us?" I asked.

"We're too far apart," my dad said. "We don't know where they are. And they don't know where we are. But maybe someday we'll all travel in spaceships, and far, far from our homes we'll meet."

"What started the universe?" Julian asked.

"That's hard to explain," my dad said. "The astronomers say it used to be small. In fact, tiny. Just one very tiny point. Then there was an explosion. It happened fifteen billion years ago. Something blew up. Something like—well, a kind of magic firecracker energy seed.

"Except—it wasn't really a thing. It existed before time and before space. Before anything. So they can't say when it was, or where, or what. They can't say why it blew up, or if some other being made it. That's why it's like magic.

"In one second, the magic firecracker energy seed made all the subatomic particles in the universe. Then the particles spent fifteen billion years spreading out and becoming stars and planets and plants and animals and people."

"So we all are really old when we're born," my mom said, wonderingly. "All the particles in our bodies are as old as the universe."

"That means we're all fifteen billion years old!" Tyrone said.

I couldn't believe it.

I'm not seven, I thought. I'm fifteen billion! I pinched myself all over, trying to feel the oldness in me. I pinched Spunky, and he yelped.

"What did you do to Spunky?" my mom said.

"I was just looking for his particles," I said.

Mom frowned. "Don't pinch Spunky just because everything is fifteen billion years old!"

"People don't know this," Julian said. "We should have a yard sale! We can sell everything as antique. We can advertise. 'Fifteen-billion-year-old family sells all!' A lot of people will come."

"They might!" my dad said. "Except we would have to tell them *everything* in the universe is fifteen billion years old. Then they might just decide the fifteen-billion-year-old stuff they already have is okay. They might just keep their fifteen-billion-year-old money and go home."

"Besides," my mom said, "I like our stuff even if it is old."

"I guess we don't need their antique money anyway," Julian said. But he sounded disappointed.

I thought of a riddle.

> *What's right here and far away?*
> *What's right now and long ago?*

I asked it.

"The universe," Gloria said.

"Right!" I said.

"It's here, and it's far away. It's old, and it's young," Dad agreed. "And everything in it is spinning and flying farther and farther out into space. Us, too."

Tyrone sat up. "If you were going to explore space, what would you take with you?" he asked.

"Universal money," Julian said.

"Pictures of back home," Shavaun said.

"Friends," Gloria said.

I patted Spunky. "A dog and a lot of dog food," I said.

"A suitcase full of memories," my mother said. "Because memories tell us who we've been and who we are. 'Cause if we aren't anybody, there's no use going anywhere."

"Myself, I'd take all my favorite songs," Tyrone said. "On the other side of the universe, I'd teach them to somebody."

"I'd take a time machine," my dad said, "so I could go back to all the best times and places."

"Stop by here!" my mom said. "Because there'll never be another night just like tonight."

"I'd come back to here," my dad said. "I won't forget tonight." Then he looked at his watch. "It's nine o'clock," he said. "Past the kids' bedtime."

"We shouldn't have a bedtime!" Julian protested. "We don't *need* a bedtime. We're fifteen billion years old!"

But my folks said it was our bedtime, all the same.

We carried our antique blankets and glasses in. Dad brought in his brand-new antique hat.

On the floor of our room, we fixed up

sleeping bags for Gloria, Shavaun, and Tyrone.

My mom turned the lights out. She said that just this one time, as long as we were in bed, we could stay up talking till nine-thirty.

We didn't talk very much because we threw pillows instead. We pretended that they were universes colliding, and the feathers that came out were star dust. Like us.

When a whole bunch of feathers came out, Spunky barked.

My dad stuck his head in the door. He said nobody was supposed to be moving around.

We said nothing was moving around, just Spunky and the universe.

"For human children," my dad said, "it's time to sleep."

"Yes, sir," we said. We were quiet. In the

dark, we tried finding the feathers that had come out of the pillows and sticking them back in. But that didn't work.

"We'll get them in the morning," Julian whispered.

It was a really special night. We never had so many friends sleep over before.

The universe is too big to be alone in, I thought. Probably even the stars are happy that they have each other.

I wondered how you knew *exactly* when the particles that made you became fifteen billion years old. I could say I turned fifteen billion the night I found out about them.

It seemed like I should feel some wisdom inside from my ancient particles—but when I tried to feel it, I couldn't.

I could just feel Spunky's chest expand as

he breathed, and hear everybody else softly breathing.

The subatomic particles that make our bodies had zoomed around the universe for almost fifteen billion years before they became us. It seemed like a miracle that they finally *had* made us—that we were all in our house together, on Earth, under the sky, among the stars.

For a minute I imagined the universe and everything in it the way Dad said it was—all kind of loose and flying around like crazy. I hugged Spunky.

"Julian," I whispered, "are you *sure* we're really here?"

"Huh?" Julian said, half-asleep. And then he whispered, "Yes."

The Treasure

On the other side of the park, where there used to be a farm, you go past a big bunch of trees, and there's a big bare place. Julian, Gloria, and I always call it the Desert. The ground is loose and sandy. It has just a few little pebbles on it and some tiny plants that never grow very much.

We showed the Desert to Shavaun and his brother, Tyrone. They liked it a lot. They scraped up some sand and let it run through their fingers.

"There might be gold here," Tyrone said.

"Gold! I don't believe it!" Julian said.

"I didn't say there was," Tyrone said. "I said there *might* be."

"Why?" Gloria asked.

"I saw a place just like this in a movie once. An old prospector made camp at it and started digging and digging. He was an old guy with a beard and a messed-up old hat. Some other guys rode by on horseback and laughed at him, but he just kept digging. And then, one day, he hit it. Gold!"

Tyrone danced around to show us how the old prospector had danced when he hit gold. Tyrone's left foot scuffed up a stone, and he bent and picked it up. It had thin crumbly sheets of silvery stuff in it. It looked valuable.

Even my dog, Spunky, looked at it like it was valuable.

"Sometimes gold is around this stuff!" Tyrone said. "The name of it is mica."

"We could dig here," Julian said. "Maybe *we'll* hit gold."

"You can't expect to hit it right away," Tyrone said. "You got to dig a long time."

"We can do it!" Gloria said. "Let's get tools!"

We got wooden stakes and a big sheet of plastic to make a camp tent. Tyrone said it wouldn't be a prospector's camp without a tent. We'd use the tent to get out of the sun and the rain, he said.

We hammered stakes into the ground and fastened the plastic to them with string. We had one tall stake in the middle to hold the roof up. When we finished, it was a good place to meet and do our planning.

About ten feet away, we scratched out a big square on the ground with a stick. Then, inside the lines, we started digging. We only had three garden shovels, so two of us watched out for strangers while the rest dug.

I didn't get as many turns to dig as everybody else, though, because Julian hogged our shovel. I complained, and Julian said he'd give me more turns later.

I spent a lot of time checking the dirt for

gold, and saving the mica and stones we found. We used a hoe to scrape the dirt back from the sides of the hole. Inside the mine, Julian, Tyrone, and Shavaun hit four big rocks. They were so heavy everybody had to help move them. After we dug around one, we'd set it on a board. Then all of us would lift one end of the board to roll the rock out of the mine. That worked, but once Spunky got too close and almost got a rock rolled on him. Then Tyrone and Julian said that when we went to the mine, I should tie Spunky up to a tree by the prospector's tent. So every day I did that, but Spunky didn't like it.

It was summer. We had lots of time to dig. We dug some every day. Deep in, we found some really strange stuff.

An old work boot with rotted shoelaces. Maybe it had belonged to some miner.

A red-and-white dish in two pieces. We could still see the flower pattern on it. It looked very old.

"The miner must have been eating something one day," Shavaun guessed. "Then maybe somebody surprised him, and the dish fell into the mine."

"Then there'd be food in the dish!" Gloria said.

"Not anymore," Tyrone said. "It would have rotted away to nothing by now."

Just the word "rotted" gave me a funny feeling. I turned all cold and clammy when we talked about it.

Down below the dish, we found a bone. We cleaned it, and it turned white.

"A bone from the miner's meal," I guessed.

"A bone from the miner!" Julian said.

We cleaned everything we found—the stones, the mica, the boot, the dish, and the bone—and guarded them in the tent.

After a week, Gloria brought a yardstick from home to measure how deep the mine was. But the mine was deeper than the yardstick. Tyrone figured out that we could let a piece of string down to the bottom of the mine, and afterward measure the string. We did that and found out the mine was three feet six inches deep.

The next time we measured the mine, it was four feet deep. We had to nail together boards to make a ladder to get down into it.

When we needed to rest, we went into the tent. In the tent, we'd talk about how far down we'd go, and what it would be like to come out in another country, on the other side of the earth.

After the mine got to be six feet deep, only Julian and Tyrone were tall enough to work down in it. But they couldn't throw the dirt they dug out of it, because the mine was too deep. We tied a rope to the handle of a bucket. When they had the bucket filled, Gloria, Shavaun, and I together hauled it up. We would check the load for gold and then spread the dirt around, away from the sides of the mine. Then we'd pass the bucket back down to Julian and Tyrone.

We still hadn't found gold, but we kept digging. We were proud of the mine anyway, even if we never hit gold. Just because we could make it go so deep, we were proud.

In two more days, we got to another problem. Our ladder was too short, but we didn't have any more wood to make it longer.

"There's only one more way to keep

going," Tyrone said. "Just one person goes down in the mine. We tie the rope under his arms and let him down to where the ladder starts. He climbs down and fills the bucket with dirt, and we haul it up and send it back down empty.

"At the end of the day, he ties the rope under his arms, and when he gets to where the ladder ends, we'll haul him out again."

"What if the person gets thirsty down there? What if he gets hungry?" I asked.

"We'll pass down a bottle of water or a sandwich," Tyrone said.

"We're strong enough to pass down a water bottle, but I don't think we're strong enough to haul anyone out of there," Gloria objected.

"We can do it!" Julian said. "As long as it's Huey who works down in the mine."

"Why me?" I asked.

"Because it's your turn," Julian said.

"My turn? Why is it my turn?" I asked.

"Because you didn't get enough turns digging before. You said so yourself, Huey. You said you wanted more turns."

"I did say that, but—"

"This is your big chance!" Julian said. "Take it!"

"Okay," I said.

"We have to do a test," Shavaun said. "If each one of us can lift Huey, for sure all of us can pull him out of the mine. You ready, Huey?"

Tyrone lifted me first. He put his arms under my arms and got me off the ground. I didn't like feeling my feet off the ground and my legs in the air. It made me feel like a baby.

But I didn't want to act like a baby, so I didn't say how I felt.

Then Julian, Shavaun, and Gloria tried lifting me, and they could do it, too. But I didn't feel good when they did it either.

Tyrone tied our thickest rope under my shoulders and tied a knot above that place that I could hold. They all held the end of the rope, and I walked to the edge of the mine.

It was scary looking into it. The bottom seemed such a long way down, all reddish sand and all in shadows. The sun didn't get down into it much anymore. Even the top of the ladder looked a long way down. I thought of saying I wouldn't go down—but if I did, they'd all think I was scared.

Julian told me not to look at the bottom of the mine, just to lie on the ground and dangle my legs down toward the ladder and they'd let me down. I let myself off the edge of the mine and the rope pulled tight. I heard Spunky start whining and barking and Julian telling him to be quiet. But it was only a few seconds before I felt my feet on the ladder, and I climbed down it to the bottom of the mine.

"Good for you, Huey!" everybody said.

And, "Quiet, Spunky!" Spunky got quiet, or at least I couldn't hear him anymore.

Our mine was nice, but it wasn't very nice to be down in it. It smelled all damp, and it scared me because I couldn't see out. But I was strong enough to climb into it, so I would be strong enough to climb out.

Gloria passed my shovel down on the rope. And then Tyrone and Julian passed the bucket down. I shoveled and sent up two buckets of dirt.

I saw their faces when they pulled the bucket up the first time, but then they stopped coming close to the edge of the mine, because the sides were crumbly.

"Good work, Huey," they yelled when I sent the bucket up a second time. But I couldn't see them. All I could see was crumbly red sandy dirt walls, and no gold, and, way, way above my head, a gray little piece of sky that looked at me and seemed like it said, "Oh, you're there. So what." I never saw the sky so mean.

"How far down are you, Huey?" Gloria yelled.

"I don't know."

"I'm going to look," she yelled.

She must have lain down on the ground

and crawled to the edge of the mine, because in a minute I saw her face above me. It felt good to see her.

"Good job, Huey!" she called. And then she said to the rest, "I think the mine is deep enough now." Her head moved out of sight.

"It should be deeper," I heard Tyrone say.

"A little deeper," Julian's voice said.

"Can you dig deeper, Huey?" Shavaun yelled.

"I can," I yelled back. Then I heard them start arguing.

"The mine is *too* deep," Gloria said.

"It's just getting good!" Tyrone said.

"It's too deep. It's dangerous. We should quit," Gloria said.

"It's a good mine and we aren't quitting," Tyrone said.

"Then—I'm leaving!" Gloria said.

The sky got darker. If I'd have been a little kid, I'd really have been scared.

"You got another bucket for us, Huey?" Julian said.

"Not yet," I said. "I'm tired."

I took a long time to fill the next bucket and the next.

"I wish we had a big ladder," I shouted.

"Don't worry," Tyrone said. "Whenever you want, you climb the one that's there. Then we'll pull you out the rest of the way."

A little gray pebble fell from the top of the mine. I watched it skitter and bounce all the way down to the bottom. And then another one fell. They were just little pebbles. Probably the wind made them fall.

"Just one more bucket, Huey," Julian shouted. "I'd look at you, but we think maybe we shouldn't go near the edge."

They weren't watching. They couldn't watch. I didn't fill the bucket. I didn't want to fill the bucket. I didn't care about gold. I sat down on the ground and pulled my knees up to my head and put my arms around them and just stared at the wall of the mine. I felt a little better that way, but I didn't know why. Maybe because I wasn't doing what they said.

I felt scared, though. I felt just like a little kid.

Then I heard the sound of running. And Gloria's voice shouting, "Over here!"

I heard Tyrone say, "Mr. Bates!"

I heard something like the sound of a board slapping down on the ground. Then I saw my dad's face looking down on me.

"Huey," he said, "are you all right?"

"I'm okay," I said. "I just want to come out."

"I'll get you out," my dad said.

He threw down the big rope with the knots on it, but I didn't move. I felt frozen to where I was.

"Stand up, Huey!" my dad said. He said it, so I stood up.

"Tie the rope around yourself," he said.

I tied it around me.

"That's good. That's tight. Now climb the ladder, Huey!" he said. "Climb it to the top."

I did. It was better being on the ladder, closer to Dad. Some more pebbles skittered by me. When I watched them, I couldn't think.

"I can't stand up, Huey," my dad said. "That could cause a cave-in. So I'll pull the rope up with my arms. While I do that, you climb it. It's only a few feet. Climb it fast!"

I climbed as fast as I could, but I was swinging in space. When my feet hit the side of the pit, big bunches of sand came loose.

"Hang on, Huey!" my dad said. "Just hang on and climb! You're a good climber, Huey. I know that."

I kept going higher. I was just a little bit below Dad.

"Shinny up the rope, Huey!" he said. "Hold it tight with your legs. Now grab my neck with your hands, Huey. You can do it!"

I held the rope hard with my legs and let go with my hands. I grabbed Dad's neck. He let go of the rope and started pushing himself up with his hands. With his neck, he pulled me above the edge of the mine.

He was lying on a wide, thin board. "Now climb onto the board, Huey," he said. "Follow me."

He crawled backward, away from the mine. He kept telling me to follow him, and his eyes never left my eyes. The light from his eyes was so strong it was like a golden bridge. All I had to do was follow it.

We got to the far end of the board, to the tent we'd made. Julian, Tyrone, Shavaun, and Gloria were standing by it with scared faces.

Behind us, we heard a sound like soft thunder.

"Part of the mine just caved in!" Tyrone said. Everybody else was silent.

"We lost the ladder," I said.

"That doesn't matter," my dad said. He hugged me.

Behind me, Spunky was whining and jumping against his rope.

"Spunky! It's okay," I said.

Gloria ran and untied him. He bounded straight to me and starting sniffing me all over.

Tyrone was looking at my dad. "We just thought we'd hit gold or find a treasure."

My dad held me like I was a little kid. He was panting.

"Here's the treasure," he said. "Right here."

Nobody said anything for a long time. Julian, Tyrone, Shavaun, and Gloria stood around us in a circle. Julian, Tyrone, and Shavaun looked like they were scared of getting punished.

"It's an amazing thing, your mine," my dad said to them. "But it has to be destroyed. A real mine needs reinforcements to make sure it doesn't cave in. It takes engineers who know how strong they need to make the reinforcements. It takes a lot of study to make a mine. And sometimes the engineers still get it wrong, and the mine caves in. If this mine had caved in, all you children could have died in it.

"I can't work anymore," he said. "You children are going to have to fill in the mine. Use your shovels and keep back from the edge."

Shavaun, Tyrone, Julian, and Gloria took turns with the shovels. It was amazing how fast the dirt went back into the hole—so much faster than it came out. I lay back against my dad, and Spunky lay on top of me.

While they threw the dirt back, I kept looking for something like gold. But it wasn't there.

Shavaun, Tyrone, Julian, and Gloria had the mine mostly filled when my dad told them to stop. He asked if anybody had a piece of paper. Gloria did.

He said we should write a message in it and put it into the mine.

"A message?" Tyrone said.

"Yes," my dad said.

And he told Gloria what to write.

"Danger! Do not dig beyond this point. P.S. There is no gold here."

And then he made us all sign it.

"Mr. Bates?" Shavaun said. "That paper's just going to rot in that dirt."

"I have a way to preserve it," my dad said.

He let go of me and reached in his pocket.

"Fold the note up and put it in this," he said.

He handed Shavaun his pack of cigarettes.

Shavaun started taking the cigarettes out of it.

"No!" my dad said. "Leave the cigarettes in the pack and put the note in and bury the whole thing."

So Shavaun stuffed all the cigarettes back
into the pack, and shoved the note into it
and closed it. He threw the pack into the
mine. Shavaun, Julian, and Tyrone shoveled
some more. Dirt fell on top of the pack, and
more dirt. Finally it was buried, and the
mine was all filled in.

It was late when we took our shovels and
bucket and stakes and our tent and Dad's
board and went home. My dad carried me

on his shoulders a little way, till he told me I was too heavy for him, and put me down. It was good to be above the ground instead of under it.

Nobody talked all the way out of the park, but when we got to the exit, Dad asked everybody to stop.

"Listen," he said. "I want you to know I don't blame anybody for the mine. I'm not going to try to get you punished. But next time, before you do a project, tell us parents what it is and get permission. Always think about what you're doing! About what could happen. There won't always be someone around to think for you, the way Gloria did today."

"Yes, sir, Mr. Bates," Tyrone said.

"Thank you, Mr. Bates," Gloria and Shavaun said.

And then we all split up and went on home.

I was really glad to see our house.

We went inside. My dad told my mom what had happened. We all had baths. We needed them. And then we ate dinner.

Afterward I wondered if my dad was going to leave to go after some more cigarettes. I knew he was out. But he didn't get up to go. He just sat on the couch with Mom and Julian and me.

"This afternoon, I felt old," my dad said. "I thought I wasn't going to make it. Running through the park and hauling that board with me. I thought I didn't have the speed or the strength or the lungs anymore.

"Huey, when I saw you down in that pit . . . That pit, that 'mine'! It looked so much like a grave!

"You all are my treasures," he said. "I'm so lucky to be with you."

Dad's voice was husky and low. One of his hands was in a fist on his knee. With the other, he took Mom's hand.

"I have some news for you all," he said. "I'm quitting."

"Quitting?" Mom repeated. Her voice sounded hopeful and uncertain.

"Quitting cigarettes," Dad said. "No more ten. No nine. No eight. None. I'm finished."

"Are you sure? It's got to be so hard—" Mom began.

"It's not hard! Don't talk to me about its being hard!" Dad interrupted. "When you want to do a thing bad enough, it's easy."

His voice got low. "What was hard was getting to this point. To this point where I'm

clear. To this point where I *know:* I don't want my false friend."

"*Great!*" Julian said. He said it softly, as if he was hardly breathing.

"And I thank you boys," Dad said, "because I don't think I ever would have got to the deciding point without you."

"We're glad we helped," I said.

"We're really happy, Ralph," my mom said.

My dad's eyes looked almost teary. He was smiling, and his arms were reaching out to us.

"I love you," he said. "My family. My true friends."

Bitol

Biten